LOCKED UP IN THE HUCOW PRISON

Steamy Milking Story

Leandra Camilli

CONTENTS

CHAPTER 1

"What brings a beautiful woman like you to a place like this?" He asked, startling me. I didn't think he was going to show up all of a sudden behind me, his hands holding an assault rifle.

Things were complicated here in the Hucow Prison, and guards like Carl were always on edge. He poked his rifle into my butt. The audacity of this man!

He pissed off me so much, even though there was no denying that I found him extremely hot. He was probably the hottest guy in the Hucow Prison, and he knew that well.

He had a huge grin on his face as though he already knew he was making me feel something deep and forbidden for him. But I was aware that nothing was going to happen between us, even though we had been becoming closer as friends recently, too.

So why did he ask me that question? He was just playing with me, and it was nothing more than that.

"Carl!" I yelled, lifting my hand and opening it. I was going to slap his face, but then I realized the mistake I would be making if I did that.

No matter how much he annoyed me, I was just so desperate I was beginning to think he might be the one. After all, recently he had been giving me weird, mixed signals, and I didn't know what to make of them.

I knew he was older than me, extremely experienced, and his looks alone made me feel some heat in my pussy. It was difficult to describe it, and I knew that it was a reflection of how much he could arouse me.

He was taller than me and his body was just so perfect. He was so dreamy. I couldn't help but glance at his lips, my eyes not moving for seconds longer than it was safe.

He winked. What a bastard! He was always so self-assured, as he should be. Someone that worked out as much as he did, that was always doing cardio, patrolling the Hucow Prison, fighting people that tried to break inside, and the like, he just had to look strong.

And it was working. I knew that most of the men in the Hucow Prison feared him, and he wouldn't have that any other way. There was always something about him that made me feel tingles in my spine, and I just couldn't stop wondering what he looked like without his uniform.

Talk about a man in a uniform, I thought with a chuckle.

His muscles, how they shifted even when he wasn't doing anything special, just holding his assault rifle as though he expected to go to war anytime soon, and the way that his skin shone under the soft, cold sunlight… Was it even possible for me to stop ogling him?

I didn't know, but it was like nothing else was happening around us anymore. I couldn't notice the other inmates playing on the basketball court anymore, the other guards patrolling the place, the walls that surrounded us, and pretty much everything else.

It was like everything was frozen around us.

"I knew you were going to say that." He stood in front of me, his eyes sizing me up. I knew there was something different between us, but I didn't think it was going to be helping him to make his move on me.

It wasn't that Carl was forcing himself on me or anything like that, but he was just dangerously close. Even though it was cold around me, the lack of sunlight making me feel a little depressed, I could still imagine how warm his body was, especially if I touched it.

But that was the problem. He would never let me touch him.

He was single, and I didn't think he was looking for a girlfriend or anything of the sort, but there was always this barrier between us, and I didn't think I could break it.

Not to mention that given that I was a lawyer – or was before being locked up in the Hucow Prison – I didn't want to appear weak in front of anyone, much less the guy that appeared to be so obsessed with me.

I swear, it was like he could only keep thinking about me.

It was good to have his entire attention focused on me, but there was no denying that, sometimes, it was also taxing.

"I know what you're trying to do, Carl," I said, smiling and peeking over his shoulder. If he thought that his machinations and advances on me were going to work, then he had something coming.

I thought that because I was a lawyer and I also knew another person from the same work field as me, and he spent a lot of time inside the prison even though he wasn't an inmate.

He was standing on the other side of the courtyard, looking at us with judging eyes.

He didn't like where this was going, especially because he promised me that he was going to get me out of here. But that was more difficult said than done.

I didn't tell him this, but I actually chose to come here to the Hucow Prison, and the reason behind that was extremely simple.

I heard that here the guards and pretty much everyone that frequented this place had high levels of libido, and I was looking to take advantage of that.

I could just imagine myself in a gangbang even though that would probably never happen.

Carl looked over his shoulder, realizing that he didn't have any more time. He took a deep breath, turned around, looking at me from the corners of his eyes, and then he said, "I'm going to be waiting for you when the place is in lockdown."

"Lockdown?" I asked, wondering what he meant, but he didn't give me much time to be wondering about that – or any time to ask him about it, to be honest. Just as he finished saying that, he walked away, leaving me speechless.

I knew that he had some beef with Charles, but I didn't think it was that bad and that he was going to leave me completely alone just outside of the basketball court because of it.

And as he walked away, I couldn't help but scrutinize every part of his body, wondering again how he looked without his uniform.

CHAPTER 2

I had to be going mad. Why was I thinking that anything was going to happen between us? Of course that it would never. But the thing was that I was here and not much had happened yet.

I was still the same person, still thinking that I made one of the biggest mistakes in my life coming here. My body was changing, I was becoming more like all the other hucows, but it wasn't enough.

I didn't come here to make milk and to be just another hucow, I thought, feeling the water moving around me and down to the floor. I was under the showerhead, and I was taking a shower. It was a steamy one, and remarkably refreshing and stress-relieving, too.

I felt like I could finally breathe again.

I was just so horny. Perhaps it was something to do with the injection they gave me. Whatever was the case, it was working. It was making me so much more aroused that I just wanted to open my legs for the first guy that would take me.

The problem was, they were being harder than I thought they would be.

I didn't know what it was with the prison guards, but they were all behaving as though everyone was drooling over them, and that wasn't what I thought would happen when I came here.

I made some friends here, though, and they were all pregnant. They always told me so many stories about what happened here when they arrived. Mary, Kristy, and Linda were all fucked the first day they came here, and I wanted to live similar stories, too.

The problem was that the more time passed here and the more nothing happened, the more I was beginning to think that I was extremely unlucky.

I shook my head, taking those thoughts out of my mind. They weren't going to help me, I thought, turning around when I noticed that there was a shadow in front of me.

For a moment, I thought I was imagining things, but then I realized that the shadow was actually a man. Had he been standing there this whole time? I didn't know, but he was looking at me with such mischievous eyes, his upper lip biting his bottom lip.

I blinked twice, not understanding what was happening here.

I checked my surroundings, noticing that the communal bathroom was empty now. When I came here, it was filled with the other hucows – the ones not too big yet and that could still walk, that was.

They were taking their showers until not too long ago. What happened here? Was it possible that this man was the one that ordered them to leave? I didn't know, but it was one of the questions that I meant to ask him.

And he was none other than Charles.

I was kind of hoping that he was Carl, but I wasn't picky. I was just happy that this was finally happening. This whole time, so many people, with so many of my friends telling me those incredible, dirty things that happened in the Hucow Prison, and I was already beginning to think that they had all lied to me.

He was hard, I noticed. I noticed the boner under his pants, and I just wanted to fall down to my knees, lower his pants, and take out his cock. I knew he was big, but it would be so different to finally have my fingers moving around his prick, to play with the skin, to love it, to move my tongue across it, and to do other things I could only imagine right now.

"What are you doing here?" I stepped back, but I didn't actually mean to do that. He just took me by surprise was all, and I never thought that he would show up in the communal bathroom unannounced, his eyes still scrutinizing every part of me.

Were we actually going to have sex? I didn't know, but the fact that he was hard and that his cock was pointing at me was making me salivate just thinking about it.

"I was thinking about you a lot, Cheryl," he said, putting his hand on my shoulder and making me fall down on my knees. In the meantime, I couldn't even think properly and even breathing was becoming more difficult.

I could still feel the water on my body when he lowered his pants. He was still wearing the suit that he put on when he went to his office. From friends to friends with benefits, I thought, licking my lips.

I just couldn't believe that I was finally going to suck my first cock, and that it was going to be none other than my friend's.

Still, I couldn't help but wonder if Carl knew anything about this and if he would feel jealous.

"On a scale of 1 to 10, how much do you want this?" He asked, showing his pair of boxer briefs. It contrasted nicely with his white skin, and I felt my breath hitching in my throat when I saw his cockhead and then the full length of his member.

And I just noticed that my nipples were leaking milk. I was already lactating, and looking at his mischievous eyes, I knew that Charles wanted that more than anything else.

His eyes were filled with lust, and he even licked his bottom lip, showing me that he didn't come here only to fuck me, but also to taste my milk. He was going to drink it as much as he could, and I knew that not even that would be enough.

He was going to empty my jugs, and that thought alone sent shivers down my spine.

"11," I finally replied.

CHAPTER 3

I wrapped my fingers around his cock, pulling down the skin. I looked up and I found his eyes, and it was as though he was judging me. I knew I needed his permission to continue this, and I got it. He nodded, giving me it.

I felt his fingers brushing my forehead as though he was petting me.

"You can do whatever you want to my cock as long as you please me," he said and I felt my heart speeding up. It was still so difficult to wrap my head around this, but I wasn't going to pass up the opportunity.

Without even thinking about it, I just started to move my hand up and down on his skin, feeling how hard he was. But even that wasn't enough, I noticed, my other hand going for his balls.

They hung low and were heavy, and I was certain that they were also laden with his milk. Just looking at his balls moving between my fingers was enough to make my mouth water.

It was difficult to keep behaving, not to push him down until he was sitting on the floor and I was all over his prick and balls, sucking them off one by one, making this last as long as possible.

In the meantime, I just couldn't stop stealing glances behind him, wondering if Carl would eventually show up and find us like this.

I hoped not. And as that happened, I moved my left hand to my breasts and I started to massage them, my fingers grazing over my nipple. They were so much more than that, too.

They were like teats. Big, engorged, and still leaking my milk.

I knew that Charles was looking at them and he just wanted so much to be sucking and chugging my milk, even though he couldn't do that right now because I was sucking him off. Or I was going to do that as soon as I was used to the size of his prick.

It was so massive, so thick that not even when I used both of my hands it was enough to feel like I had full control of this. I couldn't even make my fingers touch my thumb, and that was saying a lot. People always said that I had big hands, after all.

I noticed that he was leaking pre-come from the slit of his cockhead. It glistened under the strong, cold fluorescent light in the communal bathroom, and it made me want to be with my mouth all over his dick right away.

But I wasn't going to do that. Not yet, anyway. I was taking my time, after all.

When I felt that he was so hard that he would blow his load on my face if I didn't do the one thing he expected from me, I took a deep breath and dove my head, finally wrapping my lips around his massive prick.

When my mouth was covering his cockhead, I felt like stars were exploding in my mind, and it was so difficult not to start to come right at this moment. And even that wasn't enough to fully satisfy me.

I wish there was someone else here so that he was behind me, his fingers playing and torturing my teats. That was why I kept on tugging, grazing, and rubbing them with my fingers, and yet… That also wasn't enough to make me fully happy.

I was moaning and groaning louder than ever, and I was certain that everyone in the Hucow Prison could hear this. And considering that they could, I actually wanted them to be hearing everything.

I wanted to show everyone, including that bitch Brenda, that I could have everything they had here as well.

Breathing was becoming more difficult, his pre-come mixed with my saliva was making this so messy and wet, and even my pussy was squirting out my arousal.

I had already gotten into a rhythm and I didn't want it to end for any reason. It was so difficult to start the pace I was following, and I just wanted to keep going.

In the meantime, every so often I would tug, play, and torment his balls, feeling how heavy they were, and also how hot.

I was certain that some time from now he was going to be blowing his load all over my face, and… I wanted something different.

I wanted him to be shooting his load inside my mouth so that I could taste how salty it was, and I was certain that he thought the same thing.

It was for that reason he didn't hesitate before putting his hand behind my head, shoving it down, and making sure that I wasn't going to move it anywhere.

After all, he just didn't want to be disappointed.

And he wasn't going to be. I was giving my all, swirling, moving, sliding my tongue over his cock as passionately as I could, making him moan and groan. His moans and groans pumped me up, and I couldn't imagine myself not doing this right now.

In fact, everything was going so perfectly for me that I knew I was going to come. My body started to get hotter, I could feel more of my milk coming out of my teats, and I could also feel how warm my pussy was. It was almost like it was burning.

And then, it happened. Like a wave that was coming and finally crashed on the shore… My body convulsed, I started to squirm and writhe, and in the meantime, Charles didn't move his hand away. In fact, he pushed my head down so that I was with his cock so deep inside of me that it was in my throat.

It was marvelous and when it was finally over, he finally let me move my head away from his prick.

I looked at it in wonder, noticing that, during this whole ordeal, he didn't come yet.

That he was reserving for a better place, where we could feel more at home, I noticed.

He took my hand and helped me up. I didn't know where we were going, but he had to be thinking that we were going somewhere where Carl couldn't find us.

Was I okay with that? I didn't know, but there was no point in even bringing it up.

His hand was strong, determined, and I was walking in the hallway, between the cells, and cherishing the fact that all the hucows were looking at me with envious eyes.

They just couldn't believe that I scored their lawyer.

CHAPTER 4

And just when I thought that things were beginning to take a turn for the better, we stopped when the speakers announced, "The Hucow Prison is under lockdown. Everyone, back to your cells. There's a virus spreading, and we need to contain it."

The speakers didn't explain much beyond the fact that the virus was deadly to us. I looked at Charles without knowing what to think. He was so desperate to make this happen that he didn't remember to put his pants and boxer briefs back on.

He was naked, and even now, when we were still standing between the cells, I just wanted to be on my knees and suck him off.

Such a pity that I couldn't make that happen, I thought.

He shook his head and then he took me to my cell, standing behind the door as the guard locked it. "I'm going to be back here as soon as I can and as soon as I figure out what's happening with the virus," he promised, but that wasn't enough for me.

I shrugged, rolling my eyes. I couldn't believe my lack of luck.

I was with my hand on my forehead, thinking about what I was going to do when I realized that everything went dark suddenly. For a moment, I thought that it was just the fact that the guards turned off the lights so that we could sleep, but then I realized that something was amiss.

I realized that the air ducts weren't working anymore, which meant that we would be running out of oxygen anytime soon.

My pussy was warm and I could feel that I was in heat. The

only thought in my mind at the moment was how much I wanted someone – anyone – to knock me up.

And when I was beginning to grow desperate, I heard footsteps coming in the direction of my cell. I didn't think much of it, concluding that it was just one of the guards patrolling the place.

It was a big, spacious room, filled with cells, and all the hucows in them were moaning and groaning, and some were even pregnant. No reason to think anything out of the ordinary was about to happen, other than the fact that the entire building was under lockdown right now. I just truly, really couldn't believe my fucking lack of luck.

And then, the guard that was coming this way stopped in front of my cell. I couldn't see who he was. All I could see was a shadow. There was a light coming from behind him, and it made it so I could only see the outline of his body.

He was with a key chain in his hand, and I noticed that he was now using one of the keys to open the door of my cell. I didn't know what was going on, but I was already feeling excited, my hands pushing up my boobs.

It was dark, it was nighttime, and one of the guards was entering my cell without saying anything to me. And that look in his eyes... I could tell what he was thinking.

He was thinking he was going to fuck me, wasn't he? I asked myself, stepping away from him. But it wasn't like that doing that was going to help me. After all, I soon found myself with my butt pressing against the wall, showing me that I had run out of space.

"I saw what you were doing with Charles," he said and I felt my heart speeding up.

He was watching that the whole time and didn't do anything about it – until now? Was this part of his revenge or something like that? If that was the case, then I never thought this was going to be happening so suddenly and soon.

He closed the door of the cell behind him and approached me as he took off his uniform. First, his shirt, then his pants, and finally his pair of boxer briefs. Seeing that, I was so aroused that I could feel my milk coming out of my teats, flowing over my belly.

I moved my hand on it, wishing that I was pregnant. I wished that I had his baby, or even Charles'.

Why was it taking so long for that to happen?

He stepped out of his pants and approached me, his hand holding his massive prick. To call it massive would be a huge understatement, I noticed. It was so much more than that. It was making my mouth water even though we weren't doing much - yet.

He approached me, putting his hands on my arms and pushing me more against the wall, making me feel so small and slutty.

I noticed him lowering his head, and I knew that he was going to kiss me, or was he? He didn't actually do that, instead moving his head until he was on the verge of kissing my neck.

I thought he was going to do that, but he actually intended to do something else. He lowered his hands and cupped my udders, pressing them until some more of my milk came out – and this time, the volume was much more noticeable.

His hands were wet with my milk, and he didn't waste any time before lifting them, showing me how noticeable that was. Even though there was barely any light in the room and I couldn't see much of what was happening, I could still see the gentle shimmer of my milk on his hands.

I could also smell my milk and it was tempting. I wanted to lick it, but I wasn't going to do that. I wasn't going to do that because Carl wanted to do something else.

And without even telling me what that was, he just started to lick his fingers, one by one, with his tongue. He did that passionately and slowly, his eyes locked with mine as he continued to do that for so long that I thought it would never stop.

And in the meantime, it only made me want to have him do something similar, but to my udders, and I was certain he was thinking the same thing.

It was for that reason that he didn't hesitate before grabbing me and then pushing me until I was lying down on my bed.

He was on top of me, and I could only wonder the kind of

incredible things he was going to do to me right now.

CHAPTER 5

I could see his massive prick between his legs, and I knew that he was going to do something special with it. He put his fingers around it and then neared it to me, making me lick my lips.

My heart was speeding up, and I just wanted him to put his dick between my lips so that I was sucking on it for hours on end.

I knew he was thinking the same thing, which was why I didn't find it disappointing when he started to nudge his dick on my lips. And then I tried to open my mouth and cover his cock with it, only for him to show me that he had something else in mind.

Carl actually wanted to ease his cock between my udders. And then he started to do that, slowly and nicely, his prick sliding between them, the skin being pulled down, showing me more and more of his cockhead.

Then, he started to roll his hips, and he was slow as he did that. He was enjoying every moment of this, his hands moving over my body and feeling every part of it.

"You like this, don't you?" He asked, lowering his head until he put my teat between his lips, and then he began to suckle on it, drinking my milk. I could feel the pressure his lips were applying to it, and it was intoxicating.

I tilted my head back and arched my back when I felt his finger looking for my other nipple. Carl didn't hesitate before pinching it, and then he drew out a little bit more of my milk, his eyes locking with mine and showing me exactly what he was thinking.

"Yes, I do," I confessed and, in the meantime, nothing that was happening here was enough to completely satisfy me.

I just wanted him inside of me, and I wanted that to happen right at this moment. It was nice that he was sliding his cock between my udders, but I just wanted something else. And if someone else were to join us, then it would be even better.

That was what I was thinking when I noticed that someone else was opening the door of the cell.

For a moment, I thought I was only imagining things, but then I realized that that person was none other than Charles, and the glare in his eyes showed me he wasn't enjoying this at all.

"I thought I had more time," he admitted before I noticed that he was already naked. He came here prepared, and it was perfect. He didn't even have to take off his clothes.

I always wondered what he looked like naked, and now I could finally satisfy that curiosity of mine. Even though it was dark and I couldn't really see his body in detail, it was still nice. His curves, his muscles, and his nipples – pretty much everything about him resonated with me.

He climbed onto the bed and I feared that there was going to be a fight between Carl and Charles, but it turned out that my fears were unfounded.

They started to talk about what they were going to do and how they were going to approach this, and it wasn't long until I was on all fours on the bed. Someone was behind me and I didn't know who it was. All I knew was that he was already with his hands on my ass, massaging it nicely and slowly.

"Gosh, your body is so perfect. We knew that this whole time, you couldn't stop thinking about this moment, and we are glad to announce that it's finally going to happen. You're going to get pregnant – with our babies!"

He said that right behind my ear, pushing his dick until he was deep inside of me. He was none other than Charles. He came here for this and he was more than happy that he was making it happen.

He was deep inside of me, so deep that he stretched my walls, and hurt me, but it was so good that it was difficult to put it into words. Not only that but also the fact that his body was so sweaty that it took him very little effort to be sliding his massive, oversized prick inside of me as though he'd always meant to be doing this.

And then, he didn't hesitate before unloading his come inside of me, and it was an experience I would never forget. His cock pulsing, twitching, and throbbing inside of me. So delightful and rewarding.

Even breathing was becoming so difficult right now, and that was without mentioning the fact that this was far from over.

After all, my other partner was still here, his hand stroking his prick, and he was going to penetrate me right now – and he was going to do that without even wondering if he should stop or not continue this.

After all, he thought that this was his calling, and it might very well be.

EPILOGUE

I was pregnant, my hand moving over my belly slowly and nicely. I was somewhere different right now. On the rooftop of the Hucow Prison and wondering how everything happened. Well, I knew how it all happened, but it was still a lot more than I thought it would be. And now I couldn't imagine myself being in a different place at all.

I was seated on the rooftop, thinking about my life and everything that happened before this moment. I was thinking and concluding that I had been so stupid when I thought that nobody here wanted me. The truth was that Charles and Carl had always wanted me, and now they had me exactly the way they always wanted.

But there was something different going on with my body, and I couldn't put my finger on it. All I knew was that my pussy was beginning to get extremely hot, to the point where I couldn't even think properly.

It was as though they were still inside of me, even though that didn't make any sense.

I could still feel their pricks inside of me, and I wanted that to happen again.

Was it going to? I didn't know, but the more I thought about it, the more I wanted them to show up out of nowhere, just like Carl did in the courtyard, poking his assault rifle at me.

He was away so sure of himself and I knew that would never change.

It was one of the reasons why I chose him to be the father

of our baby. Or maybe *babies*, to be more precise about it. I had duplets inside of me, and it was one of the things that made me so happy right now.

I lost my V-card that infamous night with them, and just thinking about it, their pricks deep inside of me, shooting their come in my pussy and turning me into their cum dump, I couldn't help but notice the milk coming out of my teats.

Thinking about it was arousing me, and that was putting it mildly.

And I noticed that someone was coming up the stairs that led to this part of the rooftop of the prison. I looked over my shoulder and I realized that he was none other than Carl. He was coming toward me with an evil smile on his face, and it was just like I thought it was going to be.

I glanced down and I found his cock. It was massive and he already had a boner. If I asked him about it, he would obviously say that he was just happy to see me, but I knew that the truth was much different.

He sat down by my side and didn't say anything for the next few seconds, and it made me feel nervous. Everything was so quiet around us that I could even hear his breathing.

It was heavy and controlled, I noticed.

I could smell his musky scent and also his cologne. I didn't know that he wore perfume when working in the prison, and knowing that made my pussy feel hotter and wetter.

Looking down at his cock under his pants, I couldn't help but feel my mouth watering. I wanted him to take his dick out of his pants, but would he, or was he doing this only to keep tormenting me and making me think that he was filthy enough to fuck a pregnant woman?

But that was the thing. I knew that he was that way and he would never change.

Then, he turned his head slowly so that he was looking at me, and I knew that he had something dirty planned in his mind. Just thinking about it was sending shivers down my spine, too.

"Lie down, Cheryl. I want to taste and love your milk again," he said and I did as he asked. I lied down on the rooftop of the building, and then he was on top of me no more than a couple of moments later.

He grabbed one of my boobs and then put my teat between his lips, applying pressure on it. He wasn't strong or too gentle as he did that, and it was incredible.

I could feel ripples of pleasure in my body, and I had to stop everything I was doing, moaning and groaning. His hands were already all over me, and the way that his lips continued to apply pressure and suck on my teats… I would never forget it.

And one other thing that I would never forget was the fact that he was extremely gentle as he continued to do that. It just wasn't surprising, really. The way that he did that, his lips suckling on my boob, his throat working as he continued to drink all of my milk.

And I knew that what was happening here was going to bring me on the verge of orgasming. And when that happened, I would feel like my world was going to end.

Breathing was becoming more difficult, and then when it finally happened, when I couldn't contain my climax anymore, it was too strong and I passed out.

As that happened, I felt so at ease with everything going on I was more than happy. I had a huge grin on my face, and it reflected everything I was thinking.

I came just from Carl suckling on my teat, and I would do this again as many times as possible.

The End

Thank you for reading this story. Don't forget to leave your review. Your feedback helps me immensely!

TEASER: CHAINED UP AT THE HUCOW PRISON

Steamy Milking Story

"There was someone I knew that was in your position," the lawyer said, looking at me with concerned eyes, even though, checking out his face, I knew that he was feeling no pity for me.

It was like he was trying to convince me to do something, but I had no idea what that was.

I was in his office and he was sitting across the desk, looking at me as he reclined in his chair. He was absolutely stunning. One of the most handsome men I had seen in my life.

One of the things I first noticed about him when I stepped inside his office was that he was so much taller than me. I could see that my eyes were level with his nipples, which was something that didn't happen often.

Most of the men I knew weren't that tall, where I lived. I could just imagine myself in his arms, feeling the heat of his body, the beating of his heart, his fingers dancing on my skin, feeling it, and then his hot lips crashing down on mine.

Just thinking about that happening was already hardening my

nipples, which was, in turn, making me blush. Dammit! I had no idea what was going on with me, but this was concerning on all levels.

Charles was most likely looking at me and wondering what I was thinking. I looked so innocent, too, even though I was anything but. I couldn't help myself. My hands were clasped between my thighs and I was trying to make myself as small as possible, even though that wasn't working well.

After all, if there was something that people always told me I was, it was that I was curvy and busty. And yes, I pretty much was. Those were some of the few things about me I was proud of and that I always rubbed in the faces of the people I didn't like.

Usually, those were my enemies. Girls from my former high school class that thought I was less than them. But then I proved I wasn't, and now here I was, talking to my lawyer, who was most likely going to give me two options - either go to a normal prison or the Hucow Prison, and thinking about the latter... I couldn't help but feel extreme levels of anxiety.

I just never thought that this would happen. I thought that nobody would find out about what I did to my enemies. Those bitches... I hated them so much I just wanted to see them dead.

That wasn't what I did, though. It was something much less drastic.

"Ms. Cisneros?" Charles asked, his head behind his hands and his elbows on the desk, looking at me as though he was thinking about asking another question, but he was going to weigh his words better this time. After all, this was more difficult for him than it was for me. "You need to think about your choices and what you can do."

And with that said, I perked my head up. "Take me to a normal prison. I don't think I want to go to the Hucow Prison."

And having said that, he took a deep breath and then stood up and went around the desk. My heart started to beat faster than normal, and I could feel sweat coming out of the pores of my skin. He was going to go behind me, wasn't he?

It was an idiotic question. I knew he was going to do that,

thus it wasn't surprising when I felt him putting his hands on my shoulders. The audacity of this man! And yet, something about the way that his fingers were pressing against my skin sent cracks of electricity through my body.

My pussy was beginning to get wet and I couldn't do anything about that. I was just hoping that his nose wasn't perceptive enough. If that wasn't the case, then for sure he was going to notice the smell of my arousal.

"I think I can change your mind about that," he murmured behind me and even though his face was far from my head, I still felt his hot breath swirling around my neck, sending ripples of arousal down my spine.

"What do you mean? I just don't want to be subjected to a place where they are going to milk me and change me so much that I would be unrecognizable."

I could hear him sniffing and I knew he was smelling my arousal. Realizing that made me feel even more concerned than I was, and I started to rub my legs together, doing everything in my power to contain my increasing arousal.

But it was all pointless. I was getting hornier and hornier by the second, and Charles was using that to his advantage.

"If you decide to go to a common prison, your sentence won't be lowered, you won't be able to see anyone you want, you won't get any money for anything you do there, and you will also live there for so long that you will come out of there completely unrecognizable. I know it's up to you, but I think that the best option for you is pretty clear. Spend a couple of years in the Hucow Prison, get milked a couple times, and then come out of there looking like a heroine that doesn't owe the world anything."

I wasn't going to deny that it was tempting, but I couldn't even think about that properly when he was with his nose almost rubbing on the back of my neck.

Then, he moved away and sat back down in his chair. He clasped his hands together on the desk and then gazed at me with questioning eyes.

"So, have I managed to change your mind?" He asked and I

finally had enough space and time to think about it more clearly. Then, I closed my eyes, thought about it a little more, and decided to choose my words carefully so that I didn't make a huge mistake.

"All right, I'm changing my mind and I'm going to the Hucow Prison, but I hope that I'm not making a mistake."

He opened a wicked smile.

"You aren't."

SIMILAR BOOKS

SERIES - FAVORITE HUCOWS

1. First Time in the Barn

2. First Time in the Pen

3. First Time in the Shed

4. First Time in the Tractor

5. First Time on the Haystack

SERIES - FERTILE ONLY

1. Bumping the Teacher

2. Bumping the Midwife

3. Bumping the Farmhand

4. Bumping the Sinner

ABOUT THE AUTHOR

Leandra Camilli's obsession? Writing dirty, steamy stories that make her readers drool. She loves her Alpha males, hucows, sissies, and futas. If you're looking for those kinds of books, look no further.

With a cup of coffee on her table and warm socks on, she writes almost every day. Leandra Camilli has featured in several top 100 categories in the store, and she publishes weekly.